THE HONEY GUMMY BEAR FAMILY

Tyshanna Watkins

To order additional copies of this book, contact:
Xlibris
1-888-795-4274
www.Xlibris.com
Orders@Xlibris.com

The Honey Gummy Bear Family

Tyshanna Watkins

A VERY, VERY LONG TIME AGO THERE WAS AN HONEY GUMMY BEAR FAMILY THAT LIVED IN A HUGE FOREST FILLED WITH ALL KINDS OF BEAUTIFUL FRUIT TREES, NUT TREES, AND PONDS FILLED WITH FRESH BLUE WATER AND ALL TYPES OF FISH. THERE WERE BIRDS OF EVERY COLOR AND SIZE FLYING IN THE CLEAR BLUE SKIES. IT NEVER RAINED, IT NEVER SNOWED, IT WAS NEVER TOO HOT AND NEVER TOO COLD. THE WEATHER WAS ALWAYS THE SAME EVERY SINGLE DAY.

IN THIS HONEY GUMMY BEAR FAMILY, THERE WAS SWEET SOUR HONEY GUMMY FATHER BEAR, SWEETIE HONEY GUMMY MOTHER BEAR, SWEET TART HONEY GUMMY BROTHER BEAR, AND FRUITY GUMMY SISTER BEAR. THIS WAS A DAY THE HONEY GUMMY BEAR FAMILY WOULD NEVER FORGET.

ONE DAY IT WAS A TYPICAL NICE WARM AND COZY MORNING. GOOD MORNING IT IS SAID SWEETIE HONEY GUMMY MOTHER BEAR SAID LOUDLY TO EVERYONE, PLEASE COME HAVE A SEAT THERE IS WARM GOEY STICKY SWEET HONEY IN THE BOWELS FOR EVERYONE FOR BREAKFAST AND MAKE SURE YOU ALL LEAVE YOUR BOWELS NICE AND CLEAN SO WE CAN CONTINUE TO BE STRONG HEALTHY AND MOST OF ALL SWEET.

Breakfast Dinner Lunch

FRUITY GUMMY SISTER BEAR SAID, "WHY MUST WE HAVE WARM GOEY STICKY SWEET HONEY EVERY DAY, FOR BREAKFAST, LUNCH, AND DINNER? I WOULD LIKE TO HAVE SOMETHING DIFFERENT FOR BREAKFAST TODAY LIKE GUMMY BLUE BERRIES." SWEET TART GUMMY BROTHER BEAR NOD HIS HEAD UP AND DOWN AND SAID, "YEAH ME TOO."

SWEET SOUR FATHER GUMMY BEAR AND SWEETIE MOTHER GUMMY BEAR LOOKED AT EACH OTHER LONG AND HARD WITH A WIDE SMILE ON THEIR FACES AND SAID, "OK YOU BOTH CAN GO INTO THE FOREST AND FIND A BLUEBERRY TREE. BRING THE BLUEBERRIES HOME AND YOU MAY HAVE THEM FOR BREAKFAST THIS MORNING.

SO THEY BOTH KISSED THEIR GUMMY BEAR PARENTS, DASHED OUT THE DOOR AND RAN INTO THE GREEN FOREST AS QUICKLY AS THE TWO OF THEM COULD. WHILE WALKING THEY PASSED BY BLUE PONDS FILLED WITH WATER AND FISH THAT SKIPPED, THEY CAME ACROSS ALL SORTS OF NUT TREES, FIG TREES, AND FRUIT TREES.

SHORTLY AFTER WALKING BY A LEMON TREE THEY FINALLY FOUND AN BLUEBERRY TREE THEY WERE SO EXCITED AND FILLED WITH JOY THAT THEY STARTED EATING THE BLUE BERRIES RIGHT AWAY. THEY GRABBED LOTS OF HANDFUL OF BLUEBERRIES PUT THEM INTO THEIR BASKETS FILLING THEM TO THE TOP WITH FRESH BLUEBERRIES, THEN AS QUICKLY AS THEY BOTH COULD RAN BACK HOME. WHEN THEY ARRIVED HOME BOTH OF THEIR SWEET GUMMY PARENTS WHERE SOUND ASLEEP IN THEIR WARM COZY BEDS TAKING AN SHORT MORNING NAP.

SO SWEET GUMMY SISTER AND SWEET TART GUMMY BROTHER BEAR STUFFED THEIR SMALL MOUTHS WITH SO MANY BLUEBERRIES THAT THE TWO OF THEM FELL STRAIGHT ASLEEP RIGHT AFTERWARDS.

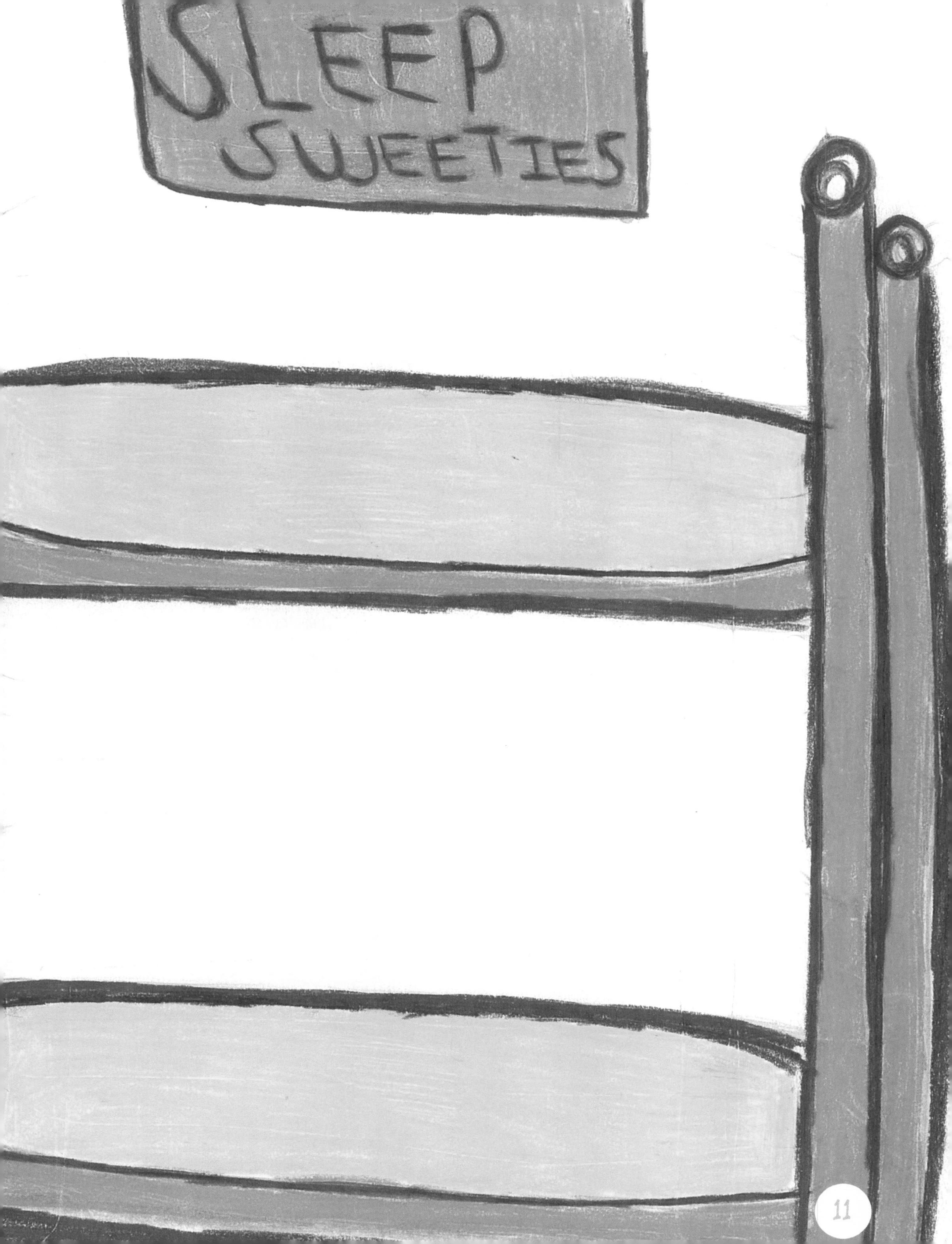
SLEEP
SWEETIES

SHORTLY THEREAFTER THEY BOTH WOKE UP AND HURRIED TO WASH THEIR FACE AND HANDS TO GET READY TO EAT LUNCH. THEY BOTH TOOK ONE LOOK AT EACH OTHER AND SAW THAT THEY WERE BOTH SO BLUE ALL OVER FROM HEAD TO TOES THE SAME COLOR BLUE AS THE BLUEBERRIES THEY PICKED AND ATE FOR BREAKFAST.

THEY RAN TO THE KITCHEN WERE THEIR PARENTS WERE MAKING WARM GOEY STICKY SWEET HONEY FOR LUNCH. THEY SCREAMED CRYING WHY ARE WE SO BLUE WHY ARE WE SO BLUE. SWEET SOUR GUMMY FATHER BEAR LOOKED AT THEM AS WELL AS SWEETIE GUMMY MOTHER BEAR WITH A GRIN ON THE BOTH OF THEIR FACES AND SAID WHY YOU BOTH ARE SO BLUE BECAUSE OF THE BLUEBERRIES YOU ATE FOR BREAKFAST.

THE SWEET HONEY GUMMY BEAR BROTHER AND SISTER SAID, "WE DON'T WANT TO BE SO BLUE. WE WANT TO BE OUR NORMAL GUMMY BEAR FLAVORED COLOR." THEY ASKED THEIR PARENTS, "HOW DO WE GO BACK TO BEING NOT SO BLUE AND BACK TO OUR NORMAL FLAVORED COLOR?"

THEIR SWEET HONEY GUMMY BEAR
PARENTS SAID, "WELL THEN YOU HAVE TO
EAT SOMETHING THAT MAKE YOU STRONG,
HEALTHY AND MOST OF ALL SWEET AND WHAT
MIGHT THAT BE THEY ASKED THEIR GUMMY
BEAR CHILDREN AND AS FAST AS THE COULD
THEY BOTH SCREAMED AND YELLED "WARM,
GOEY, STICKY, SWEET HONEY!!!"

"YES THAT'S RIGHT", SAID GUMMY MOTHER
AND FATHER BEAR.

SO FRUITY GUMMY SISTER BEAR AND SWEET TART HONEY GUMMY BROTHER BEAR ATE UP ALL THEIR WARM GOEY STICKY SWEET HONEY AS FAST AS THEY COULD AND THEY HAD EATEN MORE THAN THEY EVER HAD EATEN BEFORE THEY EVEN LICKED THEIR BOWELS CLEAN AND UNTIL THEIR STOMACHS WERE SO FULL THAT THEY FELL FAST ASLEEP IN THEIR CHAIRS AT THE TABLE WHEN THEY BOTH WOKE UP THAT EVENING THEY WERE BACK TO THEIR NORMAL SWEET GUMMY BEAR COLOR FLAVORS AGAIN AND FROM THAT DAY ON THEY ATE REMEMBERED WHAT THEIR PARENTS TOLD THEM ABOUT WARM GOEY STICKY SWEET HONEY AND HAPPILY ATE THEIR WARM GOEY STICKY SWEET HONEY EVERYDAY FOR BREAKFAST LUNCH AND DINNER SO THAT THEY WOULD REMAIN STRONG HEATHY AND MOST OF ALL SWEET.

THE END

CPSIA information can be obtained
at www.ICGtesting.com
Printed in the USA
BVHW02082625O619
551795BV00025B/76/P